The Case of the
Missing Girl

THE ANDERSON TWINS

The Case of the Missing Girl

Christa Banks

ARPress
45 Dan Road Suite 36
Canton MA 02021

Hotline: 1(800) 220-7660
Fax: 1(855) 752-6001

Ordering Information:
Quantity Sales. Special discounts are available on quantity purchases by corporations, associations, and others. For details, contact the publisher at the address above.

Printed in the United States of America.

ISBN-13   Paperback   979-8-89389-408-0
                      eBook   979-8-89389-409-7

Library of Congress Control Number: 2024916581

Dedicated to my good friend
Louise Edgington
February 24, 1927- February 14, 2010

Chapter 1

It was a beautiful spring Monday morning in Colorado Springs. The birds were singing and the squirrels were playing among the trees. Sixteen-year-old twins Shelby (a pretty girl with shoulder-length light-brown hair and green eyes) and Daniel (a handsome boy with dark- brown hair and brown eyes) were sitting in their sunroom discussing their first case. They worked as junior detectives at the police department.

Shelby took a drink of her orange juice before saying, "We really need to do something about this missing six- year-old girl."

"I smell pancakes!" remarked Daniel. Then he ran out of the sunroom.

"That boy!" Shelby said to herself as she got up to go to the kitchen. "He is always thinking about his stomach."

As they sat down at the kitchen table, their mother (a pretty woman in her forties with light-brown hair, with a little bit of gray, and green eyes) brought plates of pancakes to them and asked, "What are you going to do on your first day of spring break?"

Daniel said around a bite of pancake, "We are working on the case of the missing six-year-old girl that has been on the news the last few days."

"Daniel," Mom said, "don't talk with your mouth full, please."

After swallowing his bite of pancake, Daniel replied, "Sorry, Mom."

"Will you tell me about the case?" asked Mom. "I have been too busy the last few days to watch the news."

"Sure," the twins answered in unison.

It was the Thursday before spring break. The first- grade class at High Plains Elementary in Colorado Springs was lined up to go back to the classroom from recess. A girl named Mindy slipped out of line and ran back outside. When the rest of the class got to their desks and sat down, Mrs. Stevens, the teacher, saw that Mindy was missing. She asked the class if anyone knew where Mindy was. The boy that was behind Mindy in the line said that she had gone back outside to get her stuffed animal that she had left on the slide. When Mrs. Stevens heard this, she told her assistant, Miss Davis, to go out and get Mindy.

When Miss Davis got outside, she found the stuffed animal on the ground not too far from the building. She called for Mindy. No answer. She called two or three more times. No answer. She started frantically looking and kept calling. No answer. The little girl was gone! The assistant ran back to the classroom to tell Mrs. Stevens. Mrs. Stevens told Miss Davis to go tell the principal, Mr. Jennings, to call the police.

They dismissed school for the rest of the week. Spring break started early, but the children were very sad and worried about Mindy.

After Shelby and Daniel briefly told their mom about the little girl disappearing, she exclaimed, "That poor girl! I really hope you find her safe and sound. Well, I guess I better leave for work now. You kids be careful today."

Chapter 2

It was a noisy Thursday in the lunchroom. The children were all excited about the following week being spring break. After all the first graders had finished their lunch, the teacher, Mrs. Stevens, and her assistant, Miss Davis, got the students lined up to go outside. Once outside, all the students took off and ran to their favorite places to play.

A six-year-old girl named Mindy Norris liked to play on the big wooden jungle gym that had a slide on it. She wanted to go down the slide, so she put her stuffed cat on the landing at the top of the slide. As she was going down the slide, the bell rang. So after she got to the bottom of the slide, she ran to line up. Forgetting about her stuffed cat, she headed into the building. When she got inside, she remembered her toy.

She told the boy behind her, "I forgot and left my stuffed cat on the slide." Then she slipped out of the line. The boy did not have time to try to stop her.

When Mindy got outside, she ran to the jungle gym and climbed up to the slide. She got her stuffed cat and then slid down the slide. Mindy was heading back inside when a strange man with a puppy in his arms came over to her.

"Hello, little girl. Would you like to pet my puppy?" the man asked.

"Sure," Mindy said. Dropping her stuffed cat, Mindy started to pet the puppy. She said to the man, "He is a very cute puppy."

"Thank you," replied the man. "I have another puppy in my van that I need your help with. So will you come with me to my van?" Pointing to a black van, the man said, "It's just right over there."

Mindy looked toward the building as she told the man, "Sure, I will help you with your puppy."

They walked over to the van and the man opened the back door. He picked up Mindy and put her in the van.

"The other puppy is in the box up by the front seat," he said. "Go look."

Mindy went and looked in the box. The box was empty. The man slammed the van door shut. Mindy was trapped!

Chapter 3

t was late Monday night. Shelby and Daniel had spent the afternoon walking the school playgrounds with the police trying to find anything they could have missed. They were home now watching the ten o'clock news with their mother. They had already seen the description for the little girl several times.

Name: Mindy Norris
Gender: Female
Race: Caucasian
Age: 6 years old
Hair Color: black
Height: 41 in.
Weight: 48 pounds
She was last seen wearing a purple and white dress.

The lady on the news said, "This just came in. Someone has reported seeing a little girl fitting Mindy's description with the man fitting the description we have for you now."

Name: Unknown
Gender: Male
Race: Caucasian
Age: 40–45
Hair Color: brown
Height: 6 ft.
Weight: 185 pounds
Clean shaven (could have some growth)

"We still do not know what kind of vehicle he drives," said the lady on the news.

After the news was over, Mom turned off the TV. She sat back down on the couch and said, "I just want us to spend some time talking together."

"I miss Dad," Daniel remarked.

Shelby said, "Me too."

"I know. I do too," Mom replied. "But never give up hope, my children. Never give up hope."

They sat together for a while and talked about the twins' father. About midnight, they all decided it was bed time. Daniel dreamed of when their father was home with them. That was six years ago.

The twins, Shelby and Daniel Anderson, were born in January 1961 in Colorado Springs. The proud parents were John and Susan Anderson. In 1971, their father was sent to Vietnam. Before he left, he bought Susan a 1970 blue Ford Galaxy 500. John wanted her to have a dependable car when he left. John was good friends with the chief of police Frank Morgan, so he asked Frank if he would look out for Susan and the twins. In the spring of 1973, an army officer came to the house and told Susan that John was missing in action. Susan told the twins about their father that night. They took it hard, but they have been brave about it since.

In 1977, when Shelby and Daniel turned sixteen years old, they became junior detectives with the police department. They worked with the chief of police, Frank Morgan, most of the time. After Shelby and Daniel saved their money, they went together and bought themselves a red 1975 Toyota Corolla. They were sophomores at Mesa Ridge High School in Colorado Springs. They were both honor students. Their mother owned a pet hospital and groomers.

Chapter 4

Shelby liked to get up early (even if she went to bed late the night before) and take a glass of orange juice to the sunroom and watch the sun come up over the mountains. Daniel was still in bed asleep. After a while, Shelby went back to the kitchen. Her mother was in there when she came in.

"Good Tuesday morning, Shelby," Mom said cheerfully.

"Good morning, Mom," Shelby said.

Mom asked, "So what do you and Daniel have planned for today?"

"This afternoon we are going to go to the police station to see if we can do anything about the missing girl," Shelby told her mother.

"When do you plan to go?" Mom wanted to know.

"We plan to go after lunch," Shelby told her.

Mom asked, "Would you mind cleaning a bit around the house before you go?"

Shelby answered, "Okay. I can do that."

"I need to leave or I am going to be late for work," Mom said when she realized what time it was. "We have eight dogs coming in to get groomed today. Four of them are due for shots, plus the other cats and dogs coming in for checkups.

Just a normal work day, I guess. Bye. You and Daniel have a good day at the police station."

"Okay. Bye, Mom. Have a good day," Shelby replied. Then she started cleaning the house.

Daniel slept till almost noon. Then they had hotdogs, chips, and an apple for lunch. After Daniel finished eating, he said, "I need to go take a shower and get dressed. Then we can leave for the police station."

"I'm ready," Shelby said, a little disgusted that he woke up so late.

"Okay, okay I'll hurry!" Daniel exclaimed as he hurried out of the kitchen. Twenty minutes later, he came out and said, "Okay. I'm ready to go now."

"Finally!" Shelby exclaimed.

They went out and got into their 1975 Toyota Corolla that they bought together. Daniel drove most of the time. When he started the car, Daniel looked at the gas gauge.

"We need to stop at the gas station and get some gas," he told Shelby.

When Daniel got to the gas station, he parked facing the building because Shelby liked to watch the people. While he filled the gas tank, Daniel watched the cars drive by. He thought about the time he went to car shows with his dad.

When Daniel got back in and started the car, Shelby yelled, "Wait! There is a little girl and a man that fit the descriptions of Mindy and her kidnapper. Look! They are headed for that black van over there!"

Daniel, who knew cars very well, said, "That is a 1976 Chevy van. Can you read the license plate from here?"

Shelby said, "No. I wish I could just get out and get Mindy."

"I know," Daniel said. "Frank said not to do anything by ourselves. The kidnapper could be armed. Okay, when he pulls out of the parking space, I will drive up behind him. Do you have pen and paper?"

"Of course I have pen and paper! I'm a detective!" Shelby exclaimed.

"Okay," Daniel said. "Get ready to write."

When they were behind the black van, Shelby wrote down the make and model of the vehicle and the license plate information. She wrote:

- *1976 black Chevy van*
- *Colorado, XBL-579*

"Okay, I got it!" she exclaimed.

The man turned the opposite direction they were going.

After they drove out of the parking lot, Daniel reached over and turned on the radio. The song "You Put This Love in My Heart" by Keith Green came on. Daniel changed the station. Shelby playfully slapped his hand.

"Hey! I like that song. Leave it there please!" Shelby told her twin.

"Well, since you said please," Daniel said, giving her a wink and went back to the song Shelby wanted to hear.

When Shelby and Daniel finally got to the police station, they went in and spoke to the receptionist.

Shelby said, "Hello. We are here to see Frank Morgan. He is expecting us."

The receptionist said, "Yes, he is. I will tell him you are here."

"Thank you," said Shelby.

The receptionist got on the phone and called Frank Morgan. "Sir, the Anderson twins are here."

"Okay, send them in please," Frank told the receptionist.

Shelby and Daniel went into Frank's office.

Frank said, "Good afternoon, detectives. How are you today?"

The twins replied, "Fine."

Daniel asked, "How are you, Frank?"

"I am doing pretty well for an old man," said Frank.

"Frank, fifty-four, is not old," Shelby told him.

"Thank you, my dear," Frank said, winking at Shelby.

Then Frank asked, "Is there anything I can do for the two of you today?"

Shelby and Daniel both started talking. "Hold on you two. I can only listen to one at a time. Daniel you start," Frank said.

"We saw—" Daniel started.

Shelby stopped him. "You mean I saw!"

"Okay. Shelby, then go ahead and tell me what you saw," Frank said.

Shelby told him, "I saw a little girl and a man that fit the description of Mindy and her kidnapper."

Frank asked, "Daniel, did you see them too?"

Daniel said, "Yes. But Shelby wanted to get out and get Mindy right then."

"I wished I could get out and get Mindy. Of course I didn't do it!" Shelby exclaimed.

Frank said, "Good. That would be going against my orders, and since I am the chief of police, you don't want to do that. Not only that, your father asked me to keep an eye on you two and your mother whenever I could."

The twins said together, "Yes, sir."

Then Shelby said, "We appreciate everything you have done for us over the last six years. That includes this job as junior detectives."

"That was my pleasure," Frank told them. Then he asked them, "You didn't, by any chance, see what kind of vehicle the kidnapper drove, did you?"

Shelby got the paper out of her purse and said, "Yes, sir, we did." She handed the paper to Frank.

After reading the information, Frank said, "Good work, kids. You are the best junior detectives I know! Well, kids, I'm sorry but I have a meeting in a few minutes. I really do want to make sure you know everything about the missing girl. Can you come back tomorrow at 10:00 a.m.?"

The twins replied, "Sure, we can be here at ten o'clock tomorrow. See you then."

Chapter 5

It was Tuesday evening. Mindy was at the house of Jesse Dawson, her kidnapper. He lived out in the country where very few people saw him. Mindy sat on the floor playing with the puppy. Jesse sat on the couch watching the six o'clock news.

The lady on the news said, "This just came in about Mindy and her kidnapper. We just got the description of the vehicle the kidnapper was driving. Here is that information."

Vehicle: 1976 black Chevy van
State: Colorado
License Plate #: XBL-579

Jesse turned off the TV and said to Mindy, "Well, Mindy, my girl, they are getting way too much information on us. I think it is time for us to change our looks."

"I don't want to," exclaimed Mindy. "I just want to go home! I want my mom and dad!"

Jesse yelled, "I did not ask what you wanted!"

Then Jesse continued with his planning. "Now with your blue eyes, we could get you a blonde wig. I will get a blonde wig also. That will make it look like I am your father and you have my color hair. I will go tomorrow and get the wigs.

Now what are we going to do about the van? The police are looking for a 1976 black Chevy van. I guess I will need to buy another vehicle. It will need to be something very different from the van."

Jesse sighed and thought for a moment. Then he said, "I heard the police station has hired on a couple of teenagers as junior detectives. I doubt they will be much help!"

"I'm hungry," Mindy said.

"You are always hungry!" Jesse said angrily. "Well, I guess it is time to eat." Jesse got up and slowly walked to the kitchen. He opened the refrigerator door and said, "Here is some chicken I can throw on the grill."

Mindy asked, "Do you have some macaroni and cheese? It's my favorite!"

Jesse yelled, "Of course, it's your favorite! It's about every kid's favorite! Now get out of the kitchen! And yes, I have macaroni and cheese!"

Mindy ran back to the living room and held the puppy. "When they find me, maybe my mom and dad will let me keep you," she whispered to the puppy. "I don't have a dog at home."

After a while, Jesse yelled, "Mindy, it's time to eat! Put the puppy in the box and get in here and eat!" Mindy did what she was told.

It was around 8:15 p.m. when they finished eating. Jesse said, "I do have some children's movies you can watch if you can sit quietly. Pick one out and I will get it started."

Mindy went over to where Jesse pointed and picked out the movie *Cinderella*.

Mindy asked, "Why do you have so many movies for—"

Jesse stopped her. "None of your business, young lady, now sit down and watch the movie!"

When the movie ended around 9:45 p.m., Jesse said to Mindy, "Go to your room and go to bed."

Mindy asked, "Can I take the puppy to bed with me?" "No. He will sleep out here," Jesse told her.

Mindy went to her room and put on the white T-shirt Jesse gave her to sleep in. Then she got in bed and cried herself to sleep.

Tuesday evening, Shelby and Daniel were in their living room both reading a book. Mom came home about 6:15 p.m.

She asked the twins, "Do you want to order a pizza and play a game tonight?"

Daniel replied, "Sounds good to me!"

Shelby said, "Sounds fun!"

Mom said, "Alright then, I will order the pizza."

About fifteen minutes later, when Mom and the twins were in the car to pick up the pizza, Mom asked, "How was your day at the police station?"

Shelby answered, "Daniel and I were at the gas station today and I saw Mindy and her kidnapper."

Daniel said, "We know what the kidnapper drives now too. He drives a 1976 black Chevy van. I drove up behind him and Shelby wrote down the license plate number. That was all we could do though. Frank does not want us to do anything by ourselves because the kidnapper could be armed."

"Did you give the information to Frank?" Mom asked.

"Yes, I did," Shelby answered.

"Good job, kids!" Mom said.

When they got to the pizza place, Mom got out and got the pizza. When they got home, Shelby, Daniel, and Mom had dinner and then played the game of LIFE. They enjoyed the evening together.

Chapter 6

On Wednesday morning, Shelby made sure that Daniel was up early so they could be at the police station by 10:00 a.m. Frank wanted to talk to them about the case.

When Shelby and Daniel went into Frank's office, he said, "Good morning."

The twins said, "Good morning, Frank."

Frank said, "I wanted to make sure the two of you know about what we found out the day Mindy was taken. We have not had time to talk much about this yet. What have you heard already?"

Daniel answered, "We know that Mindy was in line going back to the classroom with the other kids when she remembered she left her toy on the jungle gym. So Mindy got out of line and went outside to get it and never came back."

Shelby said, "We don't really know what was found on the playground that day. Did Mindy have her toy when she was taken?"

"No. Mindy did not have her toy when she was taken. It was found on the ground near the building," Frank told them.

"What was the toy?" Shelby asked.

Frank said, "It was a stuffed cat. Dog hair was found on it. So we know the man had a dog with him."

"Mindy did not have a dog at home?" asked Daniel.

"No," Frank told them, "her mom and dad said they don't have a dog at home.

They said she likes dogs. She and her older brother have been asking for one for a while."

"Who found the stuffed cat?" asked Shelby.

Frank said, "The teacher's assistant, Miss Davis, found the toy on the playground. She could hardly talk to the police, she was so upset."

"That poor woman!" Shelby exclaimed, feeling sorry for Miss Davis.

Remembering something else, Frank said, "Oh, there was a purple hair ribbon found on the parking lot. The police asked around the school and nobody claimed it. One of the girls in Mindy's class said Mindy had it in her hair. She was wearing a purple dress the day she was taken. Okay, let me see if there is anything else in this folder I need to tell you about Mindy."

Frank found the paper in the folder that Shelby wrote the information on about the van. As he picked it up, Frank remarked, "Good job on getting this license plate number yesterday."

The twins said in unison, "Thank you."

Frank asked, "Do you have any more questions for me before I put you to work?"

Shelby said, "No. I think I'm good."

Daniel said, "No. I'm good too."

Jesse Dawson got up Wednesday morning and got ready to do his errands. He got out cereal and milk for himself and for Mindy.

"I have places I need to go today," Jesse told Mindy.

"I know. You are going to get wigs and a new car," Mindy said.

"Don't interrupt me while I am trying to tell you something!" yelled Jesse. "While I am gone, you are going to be locked in your bedroom. You have a TV and a bathroom in there. I will give you some snacks to have in there. You will be fine."

Mindy said, "There is not a window in there for me to look out."

"Look out a window when I get home!" Jesse told her.

"Can I have the puppy in there with me?" Mindy asked.

"Yes, you can have the puppy with you," Jesse said, getting very tired of that question.

"Do you want to know why I kidnapped you?" Jesse asked.

"Yes, why?" asked Mindy.

Jesse said, "I kidnap children to sell to couples that either can't have one of their own or their child died. The couple you are going to lost their six-year-old daughter in a car wreck and want to get another little girl the same age. Now you know why I have all those children's movies."

Mindy started crying and said, "I want to go home to my mom and dad!"

Jesse yelled, "I did not ask what you wanted!"

Jesse went to the kitchen to get Mindy some snacks and juice boxes to have in the room with her. When he came back into the living room, Jesse said, "You are going to make me a lot of money, young lady! Okay, it is time for me to go, so get the puppy and go to your room."

Still crying, Mindy asked, "When are they coming for me?"

Jesse said, "As soon as I call them and set a time and place to meet. Maybe tomorrow. I will try and call them later today. Now you be a good girl while I'm gone. Bye-bye."

He closed the door and locked it from the outside. Before Jesse left the house, he put his hat and sunglasses on so no one would recognize him.

Jesse had borrowed a car from a very close friend so he could do his errands and no one would recognize the black van. He was meeting two close friends at the car dealership.

First, Jesse went to the wig shop. He picked a blonde wig that was for a little girl and then he picked a blonde wig for himself. Jesse found that the wig shop also had mustaches. He thought a mustache would help with his disguise, so he got one.

Then Jesse went to meet his friends at the car dealership. They walked around looking at the cars for a while. Finally, Jesse decided to go for a test drive in a white 1975 Morris Marina with the salesman and decided to get the car. He went inside the car dealership with the salesman and paid cash for the car. Jesse returned the car keys to his friend and then headed for home in his new car.

When Jesse got home, he went and unlocked Mindy's bedroom door. When he opened the door, Jesse saw that Mindy was asleep. So he left the door open and went to the living room to try to call the couple that he was planning to sell Mindy to. Jesse found the number and dialed it.

"Hello," a man answered.

"Hello, Mr. Lewis. This is Mike Ferrell," Jesse said, not wanting to use his real name. "I talked to you and your wife a couple of weeks ago about finding a six-year-old girl for you. I found one about a week ago."

Mr. Lewis exclaimed, "Oh, very good, Mr. Ferrell! We have the money all ready for you."

Jesse asked, "Can we meet some place tomorrow so you can get the girl?"

Mr. Lewis said, "I can't tomorrow. My wife is out of town and will not be back until tomorrow night. She said before she left if I heard from you not to get our new little girl until she got back because she really wants to be there when the girl is delivered to us. So could we make it Friday afternoon?"

Jesse answered, "Sure. Friday will work. Bring $150,000 with you in a bag or something you can just hand over to me. I don't want to flash all that cash around. Oh! Just to let you know, she does have dark hair like you wanted, but when we meet you on Friday, she will have a blonde wig on and so will I."

Mr. Lewis said, "Okay, that sounds good."

Then Mr. Lewis asked, "Where should we meet on Friday?"

Jesse asked, "How about America the Beautiful Park Playground at four o'clock?"

Mr. Lewis answered, "That sounds good. Thank you, Mr. Ferrell. See you on Friday."

Jesse said, "Okay, see you then. Bye."

Jesse hung up the phone and saw Mindy standing there by the couch looking at him.

"I was just talking to your new daddy. You will meet him and your new mommy on Friday," Jesse told her.

"I want my own mom and dad, and my brother!" exclaimed Mindy.

Surprised, Jesse asked, "You have a brother? What is his name?"

Mindy said, "His name is Josh."

"How old is he?" asked Jesse.

Mindy told him, "Josh is ten years old."

"I see. You did not tell me you had a brother," Jesse said, very interested in this information.

Mindy yelled, "You leave my brother alone! I want to go home to my family!"

Jesse yelled, "You are not going home to your family! Go pick out a movie you want to watch and go sit down."

Mindy picked the movie *Song of the South* and handed it to Jesse. She got the puppy and went over and sat down in the big chair, and Jesse got the movie started.

That same evening, Susan got home around 6:15 p.m. from working at the pet hospital and groomers.

She called out to the twins, "Shelby and Daniel, I'm home!"

Shelby and Daniel came out to the living room to greet their mother.

"Hi, Mom," the twins said.

"How was work today?" Shelby asked.

"It was busy today," their mother told them. Then she asked, "Are you going to youth group tonight?"

"Yes, we will leave about six thirty," Daniel told her.

"Did you get something to eat?" Mom asked.

Shelby told her, "Yes, both of us had a sandwich, and we are having pizza there after the meeting."

"That sounds good," Mom replied. Then she said to the twins, "When you're at youth group tonight, why don't you ask for prayer for Mindy to be found safe and sound."

Shelby said, "We plan to."

"We need to leave if we are going to have time to talk to our friends before the meeting starts," Daniel said.

"Drive carefully," Mom said to Daniel.

Daniel replied, "I will, Mom."

"Bye, Mom," Shelby said.

When they got to the church, Shelby started to talk to her friend Bethany.

Knowing all about Shelby and Daniel working on Mindy's case with the police, Bethany asked, "How are things going with Mindy's case? Have you come up with anything yet?"

Shelby replied, "We saw the kidnapper and Mindy yesterday at the gas station. But Frank, the chief of police, told us not to do anything on our own because the kidnapper could be armed. But we did get the description of the van and the license plate number."

Bethany said, "That was good. Did you give…?"

Just then the music started. It was so loud they could not hear each other.

The youth group had praise and worship for about thirty minutes. Then Pastor Carson asked if anyone had any prayer requests. Shelby raised her hand and Pastor Carson said, "Yes, Shelby?"

Shelby said, "My brother and I have been working with the police to find a missing girl named Mindy, and we would like prayer for her safe return."

Pastor Carson replied, "I heard about that little girl. We will definitely pray for Mindy. Any more prayer requests tonight?"

A few more hands went up. After Pastor Carson heard all the requests he said, "Let us lift up these request to God for He cares about all of them."

After he prayed, Pastor Carson spoke on how God answers prayers in His own timing. After the meeting, they all had pizza and visited with each other.

Shelby and Daniel got home about 10:00 p.m. They sat down in the living room with their mother and talked for a while. They liked to talk about their father. Before they went to bed, they prayed for their father and the case the twins were working on. They prayed that God would be with Mindy and help her to be brave. Their mother prayed that no harm would come to her children while they worked with the police.

Around midnight, their mother said, "Okay, my children, it is late, and it is time for all of us to go to bed. I love you both so much. Good night."

Shelby said, "Love you too, Mom."

"Good night, Mom," Daniel said.

Chapter 7

On Thursday morning, Susan was in the kitchen making a cup of coffee for herself when Shelby came in and said, "Good morning, Mom."

Susan said, "Good morning, Shelby. How are you doing this fine morning?"

"I'm fine," Shelby sighed. "I just wish we would find Mindy."

Susan replied, "My daughter, you just need to trust God about Mindy."

Just then the phone rang. Shelby answered it. "Hello." "Hello. Is this Susan Anderson?" a woman on the phone asked.

Shelby replied, "No. This is Shelby Anderson."

The woman asked, "Is Mrs. Anderson there, please?" "Yes, she's here." Shelby said. "Hold on just a minute."

Shelby turned to her mother and said, "Mom, you have a phone call."

Susan took the phone from Shelby and said, "Hello."

The woman on the phone asked, "Are you Susan Anderson, wife of John Anderson who has been missing in action since the Vietnam War?"

Susan answered, "Yes, I am John Anderson's wife."

The woman said, "Mrs. Anderson, I am honored to be the one to tell you that your husband has been found alive and will be home in about a week."

Susan could not say anything, she had to let the news sink in. The woman asked, "Mrs. Anderson, are you there? Are you alright?"

Susan answered, "Yes, I'm here. He has been gone for so long, that to finally hear that he is coming home…"

The woman on the phone said, "Yes, Mrs. Anderson, I do understand. I waited a long time to hear about my son. He also was found alive and will be home soon. I am very happy for your family, Mrs. Anderson."

Susan said to the woman, "I am happy for you about your son coming home."

The woman on the phone replied, "Thank you, Mrs. Anderson. Have a good day."

Susan said, "You have a good day too. Goodbye."

Susan turned around and did not see Shelby in the kitchen now so she called out, "Shelby! Come in the kitchen!"

Susan had tears in her eyes when Shelby came in. "Mom, what's wrong?" Shelby asked.

Susan said to her daughter, "Shelby, they found your father alive! He will be home in about a week!"

They just cried and held each other. Susan said over and over, "Thank you, Lord, thank you, Lord!"

Daniel walked in the kitchen and saw his mother and sister crying and holding each other.

"What's going on in here? Is something wrong?" Daniel asked.

Susan turned to face Daniel and said, "Son, they found your father alive! He will be home in about week!"

Then Susan went over to her weeping son and they held each other. Daniel said, "I thought we would never see Dad again!"

Susan said, "I know. God has come through for us once again."

After a little while, Susan looked at the time and said, "Well, my children, I am late for work. I will see you tonight."

Later that afternoon, Shelby and Daniel went to the police station to see Frank. They talked to the secretary at the front desk who then called Frank and told him they were there.

When they got to his office Daniel exclaimed, "Frank, Dad has been found alive and will be home in about a week!"

Frank said, "That's great! I am happy for you. I can't wait to see him myself."

On Thursday, Jesse Dawson and Mindy were just staying at the house that day. Mindy watched another movie that Jesse had for children. She picked out *Lady and the Tramp*. Then later that night, she watched *Willy Wonka and the Chocolate Factory*.

After that, Jesse said, "Mindy, it's time for you to go to bed. Tomorrow is a big day for you. You are going to meet your new parents. Aren't you excited?"

Mindy looked at him and yelled, "No! I want to go home to my own family! You are a bad man!"

Then Mindy ran to her room, and went to bed. She cried herself to sleep like most nights since she had been kidnapped.

Chapter 8

It was about ten Friday morning when Jesse went in to wake Mindy up and said, "You need to get up so you can take a bath and get dressed. Can you wash your hair by yourself?"

Mindy said, "Yes, I can wash my hair all by myself!"

"Well, your new mother will be so pleased!" Jesse said.

"I will run your bath water for you."

"I can do it myself!" Mindy told him.

"Okay! Then get in there and get it done!" Jesse yelled. Mindy went in and did what she was told.

When Mindy went back to the living room, Jesse gave her some cold cereal and told her, "Pick out a movie and sit down and eat your cereal while you watch the movie."

Mindy picked *The Jungle Book* and handed it to Jesse. Then she went over and sat down on the floor at the coffee table and ate her cereal.

After the movie, she played with the puppy until Jesse said, "Mindy, it is three o'clock. It's time to leave for the park to meet your new parents."

Before they left the house, Jesse put Mindy's wig on her and put the leash on the puppy. Jesse already had his wig and mustache on. Then they went and got into his new car and went to the America the Beautiful Park.

POLICE

When they got there Jesse said, "Mindy, go play, but make sure you keep your wig on."

After Shelby and Daniel worked on some things for Frank, he said, "It is such a beautiful day outside, I think we should go to America the Beautiful Park and walk around for a while."

When they got there, they walked around and enjoyed the mountains around them. After a while they went and sat down on a bench by the playground to watch the children play.

Then suddenly Shelby exclaimed, "Frank, look! It looks like Mindy over there! The kidnapper is making her put a wig back on! He is wearing a wig too!"

Frank said, "Come with me. When we get to them, I will talk to the man. We need to make sure he is the kidnapper. Daniel, you stay with me. Shelby, you take the girl and talk to her. Make sure she is Mindy."

As they got to the man and the girl Frank asked, "Sir, is everything alright here?"

The man took off running. Frank exclaimed, "Daniel, come on!"

Shelby took the little girl by the hand. She asked the girl, "Are you Mindy Norris?"

The girl said, "Yes."

Then she asked, "Who are you?"

Shelby replied, "I am Shelby Anderson. My brother Daniel and I have been working with the police to find you and get you back to your family."

Mindy started to cry. Shelby held the girl and said, "You're safe now. Everything will be all right. We will take you to the police station and call your parents."

Mindy asked, "Can I take the puppy with me?"

Shelby said, "Yes. You can take the puppy to the station with you."

Frank and Daniel came back with Jesse Dawson in handcuffs. Two other police officers were with them. They were in the park nearby and joined the chase and together the four of them caught Jesse. Then they all headed back to the police station. Frank questioned Jesse. Jesse told him he was going to sell Mindy for $150,000 to a couple who lost their own daughter. They wanted him to find a six-year-old girl with dark hair and blue eyes. They were meeting him at the park to make the exchange. Jesse said he did not know anything else about the couple. Frank asked how he contacted the couple. Jesse gave Frank the phone number. Frank called one of his detectives to his office. He gave the detective the phone number and told him to track the couple down and bring them in. Frank then told the police officers that stood nearby to get Jesse out of his sight and into a cell.

Shelby and Daniel sat with Mindy as they waited for her parents to get there. Mindy had the puppy in her lap.

As she colored pictures, Mindy said, "I am hoping that my mommy and daddy will let me keep the puppy."

Shelby said, "Well, you will have to ask them."

Daniel said, "Maybe they will let you."

Frank went to his office to call Mindy's parents. He found the number and dialed it. The phone rang and a woman answered, "Hello."

"Hello, Mrs. Norris?" Frank asked.

"Yes. This is Mrs. Norris," the woman answered.

Frank said, "This is Frank Morgan, the chief of police at the Colorado Springs Police Department. I am pleased to tell you that we have caught your daughter's kidnapper, and we have Mindy safe and sound here at the station. You can come and get her now. She's very excited about seeing her family. Mindy was about to be sold to another couple who wanted a six-year-old daughter. We don't have them yet, but we will soon. So you don't need to worry about them. They don't know where Mindy lives or where she goes to school."

Mrs. Norris was crying as she said, "Oh, thank you so much for finding our daughter! We were afraid we would never see her again! I will call my husband at work and we will be there in about an hour."

Frank replied, "Alright, we will have her here at the station. We had sixteen-year-old twins helping us find her. They are Shelby and Daniel Anderson. They are with Mindy now, so she will be fine until you get here. Goodbye, Mrs. Norris."

"Goodbye and thank you so much!" Mrs. Norris exclaimed.

About an hour later the Norris family was at the police station. The secretary took them to Frank's office.

"Hello. I am Frank Morgan, chief of police. I will take you in now to see your daughter."

When Mindy saw them, she got up and ran to them crying, "Mommy, Daddy!"

They took their little girl in their arms and held her close. Then her ten-year-old brother came in to see her.

Mindy cried, "Josh!" and ran to her big brother.

"Hey, little sister!" Josh said as he gave Mindy a big hug.

Then Mindy went over to Shelby, who was holding the puppy. She took the puppy from Shelby and went back over to her parents and said, "This puppy was with the kidnapper, but he is in jail now. So the puppy does not have anyone now. Could we keep him?"

Mr. and Mrs. Norris looked at each other then said to Mindy, "Yes, we can keep the puppy."

Mindy said excitedly, "Oh, thank you, Mommy and Daddy!" Then she turned to Josh and said, "Josh we have a puppy!"

Josh said, "Cool!"

Then Mr. and Mrs. Norris went over to Shelby and Daniel and said, "Thank you so much for helping the police find our Mindy," and then gave them each a hug. Mindy went over to Shelby and threw her arms around her neck and said, "I love you, Shelby."

Shelby said, "I love you too."

Then the happy family and puppy went home.

When Shelby and Daniel got home their mother was already there. They found her in the living room relaxing with a good book.

Shelby said, "Hi, Mom."

Mom replied, "Oh hi, kids. I didn't hear you come in." Then she asked the twins, "How was your day today?" "Fine," Shelby said.

"Guess what!" exclaimed Daniel.

Mom said, "I have no idea what so ever."

"We found Mindy!" Shelby said excitedly.

Daniel remarked, "She is back home now with her family."

Mom proudly said, "That's great kids!"

Daniel exclaimed, "This has been some spring break! We found out Dad is alive and will be home soon, and Mindy is safe and sound with her own family!"

Mom said, "That's what happens when we keep our faith in God about things in our lives. It could take a short time to get an answer to our prayers. Finding Mindy took a week. Or it could take a long time to get an answer to our prayers. It took six years to find your dad, and now he will be home in about a week. We just have to remember God will always come through for us. Well kids, I think we should do something to celebrate tonight. Let's go see the movie *Freaky Friday* with Jodie Foster and Barbara Harris."

"I heard that is a funny movie," Shelby said.

Daniel remarked, "Sounds like fun."

Mom said, "Alright then, let's go out and enjoy the evening together."

And they did.

Epilogue

The next day, the detective that Frank sent to find the couple that Jesse Dawson was going to sell Mindy to went into Frank's office and said, "Sir, I brought the couple in that was going to buy Mindy Norris from Jesse Dawson. Their names are Dean and Clare Lewis."

Frank said, "Good work, Detective. Send them in here, please."

In a few minutes, Dean and Clare Lewis came in with two police officers.

"Have a seat Mr. and Mrs. Lewis," Frank told the couple. To the officers Frank said, "Officers, I would like for you to stay in here while I speak with the Lewises."

The police officers replied, "Yes, sir." They stood back by the door ready in case the Lewises tried to escape.

Frank said, "Tell me what you know about Jesse Dawson." "We don't know anything about a Jesse Dawson,"

Dean answered.

"He said you were going to buy a little girl named Mindy from him," Frank said.

Dean exclaimed, "We don't know what you are talking about! We don't know a Jesse Dawson or a little girl named Mindy!"

Frank said, "He said you were meeting him at the America the Beautiful Playground to make the exchange. You were going to pay $150,000 for the girl."

"We don't know what you're talking about!" exclaimed Dean.

Clare said, "We don't know anything about this!"

Frank said, "Jesse Dawson gave me your phone number! Stop lying to me!"

"Okay, okay!" Dean exclaimed. "We know Jesse Dawson. We were going to buy a girl named Mindy for $150,000. We were meeting at America the Beautiful Playground to make the exchange."

"Did you know where he got Mindy? Did you know he kidnapped her?" Frank asked the couple.

Dean answered, "We did not know where he got her. We didn't know anything about the girl. We knew he kidnapped her for us."

"Then you are as guilty as Jesse Dawson. You will be spending some time in jail," Frank told them.

Dean got up out of his chair and ran for the door. The officers by the door grabbed him and took him back to his chair.

Frank told the officers, "Get these two out of here, and get them into a cell."

The officers went over to the Lewises and handcuffed them.

One of the officers said to the Lewises, "You have the right to remain silent. If you do say anything, what you say can be used against you…"

That was all Frank heard because the officers left the office with the Lewises and closed the door behind them.

Frank said to himself, "Well, that is a happy ending to this case! I couldn't have done it without the Anderson twins. I am really proud of those kids! They will become great detectives someday!"

The End

About the Author

Christa Banks resides in Edmond Oklahoma with Ken, her beloved husband, and their two canine children, a cocker spaniel named Sri, and a Havanese-poodle mix named Chloe.

Christa is close to her parents and spends time helping them two or three days a week.

Christa and Ken are very active in their church. They go to Edmond Free Methodist Church where Christa's father pastored for about eleven years before retiring.

Christa has done five cross-stitch pictures over fourteen years (two of them took her five years each because she did not have a lot of time to work on them). After she finished her fifth picture, she decided to write *The Anderson Twins* and found she really enjoyed writing.

9 7 9 8 8 9 3 8 9 4 0 8 0